The Tale of the Mandarin Ducks

KATHERINE PATERSON

The Tale of the Mandarin Ducks

ILLUSTRATED BY

LEO & DIANE DILLON

SCHOLASTIC INC.   New York   Toronto   London   Auckland   Sydney

Long ago and far away in the Land of the Rising Sun, there lived together a pair of mandarin ducks. Now, the drake was a magnificent bird with plumage of colors so rich that the emperor himself would have envied it. But his mate, the duck, wore the quiet tones of the wood, blending exactly with the hole in the tree where the two had made their nest.

One day while the duck was sitting on her eggs, the drake flew down to a nearby pond to search for food. While he was there, a hunting party entered the woods. The hunters were led by the lord of the district, a proud and cruel man who believed that everything in the district belonged to him to do with as he chose. The lord was always looking for beautiful things to adorn his manor house and garden. And when he saw the drake swimming gracefully on the surface of the pond, he determined to capture him.

The lord's chief steward, a man named Shozo, tried to discourage his master. "The drake is a wild spirit, my lord," he said. "Surely he will die in captivity." But the lord pretended not to hear Shozo. Secretly he despised Shozo, because although Shozo had once been his mightiest samurai, the warrior had lost an eye in battle and was no longer handsome to look upon.

The lord ordered his servants to clear a narrow way through the undergrowth and place acorns along the path. When the drake came out of the water, he saw the acorns. How pleased he was! He forgot to be cautious, thinking only of what a feast they would be to take home to his mate.

Just as he was bending to pick up an acorn in his scarlet beak, a net fell over him, and the frightened bird was carried back to the lord's manor and placed in a small bamboo cage.

The lord was delighted with his new pet. He ordered a feast to be prepared and invited all the wealthy landowners from miles around, so that he could show off the drake and brag about his wonderful plumage, which was indeed more beautiful than the finest brocade.

But the drake could think only of his mate sitting alone on her eggs, not knowing what had happened to her husband.

As the days wore on, his crested head began to droop. His lovely feathers lost their luster. His proud, wild cry became first a weary *cronk* and then he fell silent. No matter what delicacies the kitchen maid brought him, he refused to eat. He is grieving for his mate, the girl thought, for she was wise in the customs of wild creatures.

The lord, who liked things only so long as they were beautiful and brought him honor, grew angry when he saw that the drake was ailing. "Perhaps we should let him go," Shozo suggested, "since he no longer pleases you, my lord." But the lord did not like anyone to tell him what to do, much less a one-eyed servant. He refused to release the drake, ordering instead that the cage be put out of sight so that he would no longer be annoyed by the bird's sad appearance.

When Yasuko, for this was the kitchen maid's name, saw that the drake had been cast aside and his cage relegated to the far corner of the kitchen garden, she determined to save his life. One night, when there was no moon, she crept into the garden. Without a sound, she opened the door of the cage and gently lifted out the drake. Since he was now too weak to fly, she carried him to the edge of the woods and put him on the ground. The drake shook himself, turned once as though he were bowing to her, and quickly blended into the darkness.

In a great house, there are always those who delight in causing mischief. So it was that by mid-morning, the news of the drake's disappearance had reached the ears of the lord. Now, even though the lord no longer desired the drake, he was furious at the thought that someone else should take what he considered his own. Immediately he called for Shozo. "Why have you stolen my drake?" he demanded.

Shozo simply bowed his head. He would say nothing in his own defense, for although he had not done so, he had often wanted to release the drake. To his honest mind, desiring to unlatch the cage and actually lifting the latch were one and the same.

The lord ordered that Shozo be beaten and stripped of his rank in the household. Although Shozo had once been a brave samurai—second only to the lord himself—he was now forced to haul the waste and scrub the toilets.

When Yasuko saw how he had been humiliated, she told Shozo what she had done and begged him to let her confess. Shozo forbade her to tell anyone. "Why should two suffer for one crime?" he asked. But he took comfort in her concern.

As the days passed, Yasuko and Shozo came to love each other, and this love shone so radiantly that finally they could no longer keep it hidden. Eventually, the mischief-maker told the lord of their love, and Yasuko and Shozo were called into his presence.

"It is apparent to me," he said, "that the two of you conspired to rob me of my beautiful drake. Until now I have been merciful, but you have taken advantage of my good nature. Therefore, I must make an example of you to all who would resist my will. You are hereby sentenced to death by drowning."

Since the lord's word was law, there was no way to oppose him. He called to his retainers, had the criminals bound, and prepared to march them to the pond for execution.

But just as they were about to set out, two messengers arrived at the gate. It was obvious from their rich dress that the messengers were persons of great importance. "We have been sent by the emperor," they told the lord. "His divine majesty has had a vision of the merciful Buddha, who ordered him to abolish capital punishment throughout the empire. Therefore, if there is anyone in your district under the sentence of death, you are directed to send him at once to the Imperial Court."

The lord was very angry at this order, angry enough to kill the messengers who had brought it. But he knew he had no choice. He commanded his retainers to march the condemned couple to the capital.

Now, the march was a five-day journey. As the days wore on, Yasuko and Shozo became very weary and began to lag behind the retainers. At the end of the third day, in the midst of a deep woods, the unhappy pair were so tired they could not walk another step. The impatient guards yelled at them to hurry and kept up the rapid pace. The truth of the matter was that the retainers, who seemed so brave, were frightened by the dark woods.

As night fell, and the darkness deepened, Yasuko and Shozo could hardly see one straw sandal step ahead of the other. Before long, they realized that the guards had left them behind. They were alone, without food or drink, in the middle of the cold forest.

They tried to stumble on through the blackness but soon lost the path. "*Ara!*" cried Yasuko. "See what I have done. If it were not for my foolishness, we would be back at the manor, safe and warm."

"Hush," said Shozo. "It is not foolish to show compassion for a fellow creature. Besides, what danger of the forest could match the cruelty of our former master?"

"I wish my hands were not bound behind me," Yasuko said. "I don't think I would be afraid if I could take hold of your hand."

"Come here," Shozo said. "Stand as close as you can so that your shoulder is touching mine. Then we will not lose each other in the darkness."

At that moment, they heard a rustling sound. The two stood still as pillars of stone, trying not to be frightened. "Ah," said a kind voice, "we have found you. Don't be afraid. We will take you to a place where you can rest."

"Who are you that speaks to us?" Shozo asked. He could not keep his voice from trembling.

"We are the Imperial messengers," replied another whose form was also hidden by the impenetrable night.

Yasuko and Shozo knew that they must obey, but they still couldn't help being a little frightened. They could see nothing in the blackness, and the rustle of the messengers' silk garments made a ghostly sound as they walked ahead. Finally the four of them came to a tiny clearing in the forest. There in the moonlight stood a hut made of wood and grass.

The messengers took Yasuko and Shozo inside. First they lit a lamp. Then they untied the ropes that bound them. Gently, the messengers massaged the servants' wrists. Each of them was allowed a long soak in a great wooden bathtub filled with clean, hot water. When at last Yasuko and Shozo were dressed in fresh kimonos, a wonderful feast was set before them.

The two servants ate gratefully, too tired to wonder how the messengers had come upon such delicious food in the middle of a forest. After they had finished eating, pallets and quilts were laid out for them on the tatami floor, and they fell asleep at once.

In the morning, Yasuko and Shozo were awakened by the smell of rice steaming and bean soup bubbling in an iron pot. But the messengers were nowhere to be seen. "We failed to thank them for all their kindness," Yasuko said. They jumped up and ran to the door of the hut.

There on the path were a pair of mandarin ducks. The drake wore plumage so rich and colorful that the emperor himself might have envied it, while his mate wore the quiet tones of the wood. The pair turned and seemed to bow. Then, lifting themselves into the air, they flew straight and swift as arrows fly, above the highest trees of the forest.

Yasuko and Shozo lived on for many years in their hut of wood and grass. They had many children who gave them much happiness—and a little trouble. But as they had learned years before, trouble can always be borne when it is shared.

Once again for
John
with thanks for
happiness and trouble shared
K.P.

to the beauty of ukiyo-e
D.D. & L.D.

ISBN 0-590-44988-5

Text copyright © 1990 by Katherine Paterson.
Illustrations copyright © 1990 by Diane and Leo Dillon.
All rights reserved. Published by Scholastic Inc.,
730 Broadway, New York, NY 10003,
by arrangement with Penguin Books USA Inc.

12 11 10 9 8 7 6 5 4 3 2   1 2 3 4 5 6/9

Printed in the U.S.A.   08

First Scholastic printing, October 1991